*Jim Henson's*

# Enchanted Sisters

# Winter's
# Flurry Adventure

**Autumn's Secret Gift**

**Winter's Flurry Adventure**

**Spring's Sparkle Sleepover**
(coming soon)

Jim Henson's™

# Enchanted Sisters

# Winter's Flurry Adventure

**Elise Allen**
and Halle Stanford

illustrated by
**Paige Pooler**

**BLOOMSBURY**
NEW YORK  LONDON  NEW DELHI  SYDNEY

First published in the United States of America in October 2014
by Bloomsbury Children's Books
www.bloomsbury.com

Bloomsbury is a registered trademark of Bloomsbury Publishing Plc

For information about permission to reproduce selections from this book, write to
Permissions, Bloomsbury Children's Books, 1385 Broadway, New York, NY 10018
Bloomsbury books may be purchased for business or promotional use. For information on
bulk purchases please contact Macmillan Corporate and Premium Sales Department at
specialmarkets@macmillan.com

Library of Congress Cataloging-in-Publication Data
Allen, Elise.
Winter's flurry adventure / by Elise Allen and Halle Stanford ; illustrated by Paige Pooler.
pages     cm   — (Jim Henson's Enchanted sisters)
Summary: When Flurry, a pet polar bear, becomes jealous and runs off to play
with the Weeds, who are always causing trouble, the adventurous Winter
will need the help of all her enchanted Sparkle Sisters to get him back.
ISBN 978-1-61963-267-7 (paperback) • ISBN 978-1-61963-297-4 (hardcover)
ISBN 978-1-61963-268-4 (e-book)
[1. Seasons—Fiction.  2. Nature—Fiction.  3. Magic—Fiction.  4. Friendship—
Fiction.  5. Polar bear—Fiction.  6. Bears—Fiction.  7. Jealousy—Fiction.
8. Sisters—Fiction.]  I. Stanford, Halle.  II. Pooler, Paige, illustrator.  III. Title.
PZ7.A42558Win 2014        [Fic]—dc23        2014005603

Book design by John Candell
Typeset by Westchester Book Composition
Printed and bound in the U.S.A. by Thomson-Shore Inc., Dexter, Michigan
2  4  6  8  10  9  7  5  3  1  (paperback)
2  4  6  8  10  9  7  5  3  1  (hardcover)

All papers used by Bloomsbury Publishing, Inc., are natural, recyclable products
made from wood grown in well-managed forests. The manufacturing processes
conform to the environmental regulations of the country of origin.

# CHAPTER
# 1

**W**inter rolled over in bed and pulled the covers tighter around her. She could feel the sun streaming through the window of her bedroom. It had to be late morning already, but she was so cozy under her layers of furry blankets. Why wake up before she had to?

WHOOSH!

In a single swoop, all of Winter's covers flew off her. If she hadn't been wearing soft flannel pajamas, a pom-pommed nightcap, and fuzzy slipper-socks, she might have caught a chill. Instead, she was just startled. She bolted upright and cried, "Flurry!"

Flurry, Winter's giant pet polar bear, stood at the foot of her bed. In one massive paw he held all of Winter's blankets. The other paw covered his mouth while he giggled.

"I'm going to get you, Flurry!" Winter hollered.

She sounded angry, but she wasn't. She and Flurry did this every single morning. Parts of the routine changed. Sometimes instead of pulling the covers off Winter, Flurry tickled her, or pulled her off the bed and threw her into a giant pile of pillows, or just laid his snout right against her nose and stared until her eyes flew open. Still, the result was always the same.

The chase was on.

Flurry raced out of the bedroom, and Winter slid off her bed to follow. Her bed was on stilts, like a top bunk without a bottom, and instead of a ladder it had a long, winding slide to the floor. When she didn't feel like sliding down, she'd swing hand over hand on monkey bar hoops that ran across the ceiling, then drop down onto her snowflake-shaped trampoline. Or better still, onto Flurry's back.

Winter ran out of her room and leaned over the top-floor balcony. On the second floor she saw a grandfather clock . . . with white furry arms and legs poking out behind it.

"I see you, Flurry!" she shouted, then leaped onto

the staircase banister and slid down, whooping all the way. She landed close to the bear, but Flurry didn't give up. He pushed the grandfather clock into Winter's path while he barreled away.

The clock fell with a SMASH, but Winter wasn't bothered. She vaulted over it and continued the chase. Ahead of her, Flurry crashed and bashed into couches, clawed holes in beanbag chairs, and tumbled so hard down the snow-covered sledding hill that zipped from the second floor to the first that he left a bear-shaped dent right in the middle. He didn't mean to cause so much damage, but he was a big bear. When he ran into something, destruction usually followed.

Winter didn't worry. She simply leapfrogged the damage and kept chasing. When she reached the sledding hill, she pulled a saucer sled from a wall hook and threw herself down headfirst. The sled bounced into Flurry's crater, ricocheted out, and spun wildly, getting Winter dizzier and dizzier until she crashed into a ten-foot-deep stack of pillows.

Winter heard bells.

In some universes this would mean she'd hit her head too hard, but here it was the sound of Winter's home fixing itself. She cuddled into the pillows and gazed up to enjoy the show. Shimmering sparkles danced over everything cracked, torn, or overturned. The grandfather clock righted itself, the beanbags sewed themselves up, and the dent in the sledding hill disappeared.

Winter's mother, Mother Nature, told stories about the Outworlders, who had to clean up after themselves when they made a mess. If Outworlders broke things when they played, the things *stayed* broken. Winter couldn't even imagine that. She was a Seasonal Sparkle, one of four unique sisters tasked with changing the seasons for the Outworlders, whom Mother called "humans." Each sister lived in her own Sparkledom, alive with the spirit of her particular season. Everything in Winter's Sparkledom suited her perfectly—especially her self-fixing home. What better place for a Sparkle and a bear to play?

Once her home was back to normal, Winter scanned the first floor for Flurry. Most of the floor held a giant ice rink, ringed by fluffy white couches and beanbags that looked like giant snowballs.

Suddenly, one of the snowballs sneezed.

Winter covered a laugh. The snowball was Flurry, curled into a ball to look like one of the beanbags. Silently, Winter slid onto the ice, but her slippered feet zipped so quickly she lost control. She kicked her legs and pinwheeled her arms until she smacked into Flurry's side.

"Gotcha!" she cried. "Let's skate!"

Flurry obeyed. He stood on his hind legs, grabbed Winter's hand, and pulled her to the middle of the ice. Winter whooped as they spun around faster and faster until they were both so dizzy they collapsed. Flurry landed on his back, with Winter sprawled across his belly. When she caught her breath, she crawled up his body until they were nose-to-snout.

"You are the best friend a Sparkle could ever have," she told him.

Flurry licked her cheek. Then his stomach growled. He sniffed the air hopefully and his eyes grew wide.

Winter smelled it too. "Breakfast!"

She and Flurry slid across the floor to the kitchen, which always knew when they needed a bite to eat. Winter climbed Flurry's back and leaped into a carpeted gondola that hung from the ceiling. Its top half was open, and at perfect snout height for Flurry when he stood tall. The table inside groaned under the weight of pancakes, French toast, flaky biscuits spread with butter and jam, and steaming mugs of peppermint hot chocolate with whipped cream. Winter ate a few delicious mouthfuls of everything. Flurry swallowed the rest. When he finished, he yawned, stretched, curled into a ball on the floor, and immediately fell asleep.

"Silly bear," Winter murmured affectionately. She jumped out of the gondola onto his back—Flurry didn't even blink—then skated to the rock-climbing wall that led back up to her room. She scaled her way up, then showered and changed into snow boots and one of her many blue snowsuits with a fuzz-trimmed hood that circled her face. Winter also wore her headband with its magical sparkle-gem right in the center. That she never took off. She even wore it in the shower and in her sleep. The headband was one of the two most important things she owned. The other was her magic scepter, which she locked up every night to protect it from the Weeds.

The Weeds were the Sparkles' worst enemies, boys who answered to a man named Bluster Tempest. Bluster and the Weeds lived to cause trouble, and they'd love to get their hands on the Sparkles' headbands or scepters. Without those items, the Sparkles couldn't use their Sparkle Powers. Worse, they couldn't do the Sparkle Ceremony that changed the seasons for the Outworlders.

Winter walked to a large chest in the corner. She

looked around to make sure she was alone, then pushed the chest aside, lifted a loose floorboard, and pulled out a plain wood box. It looked bland on the outside. That was on purpose. When she touched her headband gem to its lid, the box popped open to reveal a stunning scepter nestled in pillowy blue satin.

When Winter pulled out her scepter, she noticed the orb at its top was perfectly blue. That made sense. There were still many weeks left of winter. In the last few days of each season, the orbs on all of the Sparkle Sisters' scepters slowly clouded over with a silvery mist that told them exactly when they needed to gather in Mother Nature's Sparkledom for the season-changing Ceremony.

Winter slipped her scepter into her snowsuit's holster, returned the box to its secret spot, then peered outside. There had been a blizzard last night. Thick snow covered everything in sight, and Winter ached to play in it with Flurry. She somersaulted to a corner of her room, then slid down a long pole that ended in the kitchen.

Flurry was still fast asleep, but Winter knew how to wake him. She reached into her coat and pulled out a giant candy cane. The minute she peeled back the crackling plastic wrap, Flurry's nose twitched. He reached out his tongue, searching for the sweet treat even in his sleep.

"You've got to move more than that if you want it," Winter said, then leaned close to add, "Come play and I'll give you *five*."

Flurry's eyes snapped open and he leaped to his feet. He gobbled down the candy cane the second Winter tossed it to him, then begged for more.

"Yes," Winter told Flurry. "But *after* we go play! Come on!"

She ran outside and Flurry bounded after her. Cold air nipped their faces, but Winter felt only joy as she gazed at the snowdrifts around her home. They rose higher than her head!

"YES!" she whooped. She ran facefirst into the deliciously cold snow. When she backed out, she showed Flurry the Winter-print she'd made. "See? It looks like a gingerbread man! You try."

On all fours, Flurry barreled into the snowdrift. He went so far that Winter almost lost sight of him, then he spun in a circle again and again.

"What are you doing, crazy bear?" Winter asked. "Are you chasing your tail?"

Flurry's circles got wider and wider. Winter could see him only each time he passed the hole he'd made to enter. Finally, he backed out through that hole with a big grin on his face.

"What did you do?" Winter asked. She walked into the hole and gasped. By turning in circles inside the snowdrift, Flurry had carved out a round cozy room, like the inside of an igloo.

"It's a snow fort! I love it!" Winter cried as she ran back out and hugged Flurry. Then she gasped. "But you know what? We could make an even *bigger* snow fort!" She gasped again. "No . . . we could make the *biggest* snow fort . . . *ever*! And we'll bring in blankets and pillows and make it warm and cozy and then we can call my sisters over and we can have a *slumber party* in the snow fort! Let's do it!"

Winter raced inside the fort, ready to dig, but

Flurry didn't follow. Once Winter realized she was all alone, she popped her head back out to find her bear curled up for a nap. He snored.

"You are ridiculous." She sighed. She moved close and whispered in his ear, "Did I mention that during the slumber party you can have all the candy canes you can eat?"

Flurry jumped up, trotted back into the snow fort,

and started digging as fast as he could. Side by side, the best friends were unstoppable. Flurry carved giant paths through the snow with his massive paws. Then Winter used her Sparkle Power—the power to turn things to ice—to freeze the newly carved walls and keep them strong. Her job took longer than Flurry's, so her bear was soon out of sight, but in his wake he left lots of snowy hallways, caverns, and chambers—the biggest snow fort ever! Winter could already imagine her sisters' amazed faces when they saw it.

That was when Winter heard something horrible: a high-pitched screeching yelp.

It was Flurry, and he made that sound only when he was terrified.

"I'm coming, Flurry!" Winter yelled, and took off as fast as she could.

# CHAPTER
# 2

**W**inter was out of breath when she reached the end of the cavern.

"Flurry? Flurry, what's wrong?"

The bear was huddled in a corner. He stared at the wall across from him, terrified. Winter patted his head. "It's okay, Flurry. I'm here."

She followed his gaze and saw a small hole in the ground. He must have uncovered it while digging. "Is something in there?" Winter asked.

Flurry shuddered. Winter thought of Sleet, one of the Weeds. Had he tunneled into her Sparkledom? That would definitely make Flurry nervous, but it couldn't be Sleet. The hole was too small.

What could it be?

Winter pulled out her scepter. "Whatever's in

there, don't do anything crazy," she said, making her voice sound brave. "I don't want to turn you to ice, but I will if I have to."

No response.

Winter looked back at Flurry—was there really something in there?

Flurry whined.

Winter crept close to the hole. Then, when she was about to peek inside, something leaped out at her! It was small, but it jumped so quickly it smacked Winter square in the chest and knocked her backward to the ground.

"Aaaah!" Winter screamed. She dropped her scepter and grabbed her attacker with both hands.

She was holding a tiny baby fox! The fuzzy white puppy crouched on Winter's parka, his front paws low and his back in the air, ready to play. His tail wagged so quickly Winter felt the breeze.

"Arf!" he barked.

Then he pounced and licked Winter's nose.

Winter burst out laughing. She got up and showed the pup to Flurry. "Are you kidding, big guy? You were afraid of *this*?" The fox scrambled up the arm of her coat, curled on her shoulder, and nuzzled her right cheek. "Awwww," Winter said. "That's so sweet."

Suddenly, Winter felt Flurry's giant head against her *left* side. He nuzzled between her neck and shoulder, leaning so hard that Winter fell over and almost landed on the fox pup.

"Flurry!" Winter said. "Look what you did! I could have hurt the little guy!" She knelt down to the pup. "You okay?"

The pup seemed more than okay. He jumped up and down but was so clumsy on his oversized baby paws that he toppled over. Winter laughed. "You're so funny."

Out of nowhere, the entire fort shook with the force of an earthquake. Rivers of snow poured from the ceiling. Winter wheeled around to find out why...

and saw Flurry jumping up and down, an adorable smile on his face.

"Flurry, you're too big to do that!" Winter cried. "You'll cave in the fort!"

She grabbed her scepter and quickly chanted:

"Keep these walls from falling in,
Make them ice that's thick, not thin!"

She flicked her wrist, and a spray of blue glittery light shot out of her scepter, turning every spot it hit to solid ice. Winter spun until all the walls and ceiling were coated and sturdy.

"There," she said. "Much better."

Winter felt a tug at her feet and looked down. The baby fox had her boot laces between his teeth and shook them back and forth while he growled. Winter laughed.

"Go get those shoelaces," she cooed to the fox. "Go get 'em."

Suddenly, Winter jumped with a yelp.

"OW! Flurry, that's my bottom!"

Winter couldn't believe it. Flurry had just chomped the back of her snowpants! What had gotten into him? Yes, he was spooked when he found the fox, but now he knew it was harmless. Why was he still acting so strangely, and how could she make him feel better?

Before she could figure it out, she heard a tiny, high-pitched whine. It was the puppy. He had his head tipped back and his snout in the air.

"Is that supposed to be a *howl*?" she asked, amused. "Do it again."

Instead, *Flurry* howled. His roar was so loud it cracked the fort's ice walls and terrified the baby fox, who leaped into Winter's arms.

"What is up with you, Flurry?" she asked. "You're pushing me and nipping me and now you nearly brought down the fort!"

Flurry hung his head low. Winter sighed. She wasn't mad at him, but he was really making a mess of things. "Just . . . hang over there and chill out a minute, okay?" she told him. "I need to figure out what to do with this little guy."

Flurry trudged to the far end of the room. He looked sad, and Winter was already planning to comfort him with a cookie party and a long cuddly nap back home, but now she needed to think. She plopped on the ground and scooped up the fox. She held him to her face and rubbed her nose against his snout, just like she did with Flurry when he was a tiny cub.

"Where is your family, puppy?" Winter asked. "How did you end up down here all alone?" The fox didn't answer, of course. He just batted at the fur around Winter's hood.

"I bet you got separated from your family in the blizzard," Winter said, "and ended up buried in the snow. But you know what? You're in luck. My very best friend in the world happens to be an *excellent* tracker. If anyone can find your family, it'll be him. Isn't that right, Flurry?"

When the bear didn't respond, Winter craned her head around. "Flurry?"

Flurry was gone. Winter raised her voice and called louder.

"Flurry?"

Then she saw it—a new, bear-sized tunnel through the snow. Winter ran to its entrance and looked inside. It seemed to snake along forever before it turned a corner and disappeared from view.

How could Flurry have dug so far so fast? And why?

"Arf!"

Winter looked down. The fox puppy bounced at her feet, eager to play.

"Oh, no." Winter gasped as it all made sense. Why hadn't she seen it? Flurry was *jealous* of the fox!

But Flurry was her best friend in the world. Winter loved him. He had nothing to be jealous about. Didn't he know that?

Maybe he didn't. And now he'd run away.

Winter raced down the new tunnel, screaming Flurry's name.

"Flurry! *Flurry! FLURRY!*"

The walls groaned, and Winter knew she'd made a terrible mistake. Her loud yell had caused an avalanche. She raced back the way she'd come as the entire passage tumbled in on itself. As she ran, she pulled out her scepter, pointed it behind her, and screamed:

"Keep this snow fort safe and sound,
Freeze it so it won't fall down!"

Blue Sparkle magic poured from Winter's scepter and covered everything in her wake. She knew she was safe when the roar of falling snow gave way to silence. Only then did she turn . . . to face a solid wall of ice. In it she saw her own sad reflection.

A voice whined. The baby fox stood at her feet. He looked sad too.

"I stopped the cave-in," Winter said, "but I cut off the only way to follow him."

She tapped her scepter against the ice, then shook her head. "It's too thick to break, and it'll never melt down here. Not unless I grab the sun and bring it inside."

Winter sighed, then suddenly brightened. "That's it!" she cried. "I'll grab the sun and bring it inside!"

Winter tucked the baby fox into her coat pocket and ran as fast as she could for the snow fort's entrance. She knew how to get Flurry, but she couldn't do it alone.

She needed her sisters.

# CHAPTER
# 3

**W**inter didn't stop running until she was back outside, where her scepter had a clear shot at the sky. Without waiting to catch her breath, she pointed it into the air and cried:

> *"Rainbow, fetch the sparkles three,*
> *I need my sisters here with me!"*

She touched the scepter to the gem in her headband, sending a thick beam of rainbow-colored sparkles from the ground at her feet high into the air. At the very top of its arc, the rainbow split into three parts, diving out of sight into the Sparkledoms of Spring, Summer, and Autumn.

The Sparkles never ignored the rainbow call. Any

second now, Winter's sisters would see the light right beside them, step into it, and soar all the way to Winter's realm.

Winter stared at the sky and whispered impatiently, "Three . . . two . . . one!"

Summer appeared right on cue. Her long brown hair whipped around her face and her green dress flapped in the wind as she dove headfirst down the rainbow. "Watch this!" she screamed to Winter. She twirled in a quadruple somersault, then leaped out of the rainbow in an explosion of yellow sparkles. She landed with her arms spread wide. "What do you think?"

"Impressive," Winter said. "*Almost* as impressive as when I did that move last week."

"Pretty sure I added one extra flip in there," Summer said.

"Pretty sure you didn't."

"*I'm* pretty sure that you were *both* impressive, and astoundingly acrobatic," said another voice.

It was Autumn, dressed as always in her orange sari, her long dark hair braided down her back. A mist of orange sparkles danced around her as she stepped lightly out of the rainbow. "I'm glad you called," she said, taking Winter's hands. "I missed you."

"Since last night?" Winter laughed.

"Any time the four of us aren't together, I miss you," Autumn said.

"I wish I could say I just brought you here because I miss you too," Winter said, "but I need your help."

"On it," Summer said. "What can we do?"

Before Winter could answer, the sisters heard a familiar tinkle-bell giggle. They looked up to see Spring sliding feetfirst down the rainbow. Her purple dress swung around her knees, and her blond hair bounced in the wind. As she glided along, she looked at every bird, every pine needle, every snowflake . . . every bit of nature. She was so fascinated by it all that she lost track of the rainbow's end and spilled out in a cloud of purple sparkles.

"Tulips and turtles, I toppled!" she bubbled as Autumn and Summer pulled her to her feet. "Sorry I'm late, but I was playing leapfrog with some froggy friends and then I realized it was only leapfrog because

I was *leaping* over *frogs*! I wondered, would it still be the same game if I played it with other animals?"

"Spring..." Winter tried to cut in.

"So I tried it!" Spring continued excitedly. "I played leap*frog*, then leap*hog*, then leap*dog*, and then you know what I played?"

"Leap... *log*?" Summer guessed.

"No!" Spring continued. "Leap*porcupine*, of course!"

"Of course." Autumn smiled.

"But the problem with leap*porcupine* was that when the rainbow came I had porcupines stuck all over me! So I had to take a minute and peel them off, and that made me wonder if porcupines ever stuck *themselves* together, bristle to bristle, to make something like a pyramid. And if they did, would it be called a *porcu-mid*, or a *pyra-pine*, or a—"

"Spring!" Winter interrupted.

Spring stopped, then cocked her head to the side and scrunched her face. "Winter, why is your coat telling me it needs to breathe?"

Summer and Autumn looked at their youngest sister like she was crazy, but Winter understood and quickly pulled the baby fox from her pocket.

"Awwww!" her sisters chorused.

"This is what I brought you here to talk about," Winter said.

"Can I hold him?" Spring asked.

"Sure," Winter replied. "So Flurry and I found him this morning, and—"

"He's so *tiny*!" Autumn gushed.

"Yes," Winter said, "and I was playing with him and everything was fine, but then Flurry started acting really weird and I didn't understand why and I told him to sit by himself while I figured out what to do with the baby, and the next thing I knew Flurry was *gone*!"

"Aren't you the cutest little thing?" Summer asked the pup. "Yes, you are. Oh yes, you are." She looked up at her sisters. "Isn't he the cutest little thing?"

"Yes, he's super cute," Winter agreed. "But listen, I think Flurry got jealous. Which is crazy, right? I mean, how in a million years could he think I'd ever love him any less?"

If her sisters heard the question, they gave no sign of it. They all bent close to the fox, snuggling

him, petting him, and playing with his tiny baby paws.

Suddenly Winter understood how Flurry might have felt ignored and unloved. "*HEY!*" she shouted.

"What's that, little guy?" Spring asked the fox. "You said Winter wants to tell us something?"

"I do," Winter said. "Quick version, before you get distracted again. Flurry ran away. I need your help to find him."

The fox puppy made some growling noises low in his throat. Spring nodded sympathetically as she listened, then said, "Snowball feels terrible. He thinks it's his fault."

"It's not," Winter said. "I was the one who hurt Flurry's feelings. I have to find him and make it up to him. Will you help me?"

"Not even a question," Summer said. "Of course we will."

"Absolutely," Autumn agreed. "And wherever Flurry is, I'm sure he's fine."

"Thanks," Winter said. "Spring, I think Snowball got separated from his family in the blizzard last night. Will you stay and help him find them?"

Snowball growled and whimpered. Spring listened, then turned to Winter. "He says he wants to help find Flurry first." She held the tiny fluffball out to Winter. "And he wants to be with you."

Winter took Snowball, who immediately trotted up her sleeve all the way to her shoulder. He pawed at her hood until it came off her head and became a perfect baby-fox-sized basket. Snowball hopped inside.

"Awwwww!" Summer, Autumn, and Spring cooed.

"Yeah, yeah, I'm sure it's adorable," Winter said, "but we have a bear to find. Come on."

Normally, Winter's sisters would need snow-shoes, but the fort entrance was right in front of them and the snow inside was well packed.

"This place is amazing!" Summer gaped as they walked through the massive lair.

"Thanks," Winter said. "Flurry and I make a great team. That's why I want to find him and get him back home where he belongs."

Winter led her sisters through the fort, all the way to the thick wall of ice.

"I made it to stop an avalanche, but then I couldn't get past it." Winter shook her head. "Guess I don't know my own strength."

"Let's see if I know mine," Summer said. She pulled out her scepter and pointed it at the frozen barrier.

*"Melt the ice with extra care,*
*so walls and roof will stay right there!"*

Yellow sparkles streamed out of her scepter in a carefully aimed beam of light. Heat was Summer's Sparkle Power, and the glow from her scepter melted a large, perfect circle in the wall. Just as she requested in her spell, the edges of the circle remained solid and strong.

"Very nice," Winter said.

The sisters stepped through the new portal and walked down the hall. They said little. Winter was too worried about Flurry to talk, and the other sisters were mesmerized by the length and complexity of Flurry's tunnel. It seemed to go on forever. Long passages were straight, then sometimes the path would turn sharply several times in a row. Other times it circled, or doubled back on itself. Always it went downhill, deeper and deeper into the snow.

"He must have been really upset," Winter muttered. "He had no idea where he was going."

She pulled a candy cane from her pocket and unwrapped it. If Flurry was anywhere close, maybe he'd smell it and come running back. When Snowball mewled for a taste, Winter unwrapped another and handed it over her shoulder to him.

"Hey, look at this!" Summer yelled from up ahead.

"Anthills and avalanches!" Spring winced. "You shouldn't be so loud!"

"You don't have to worry up here," Summer said. "Come look."

When the other Sparkles caught up with her, they realized she was right. There was no chance of an avalanche, because there was no more snow. There wasn't even a bear-carved passageway anymore. The passageway had spilled them out into a giant, dirt-packed cavern. Scattered wood beams were strewn everywhere. Some of them leaned against the walls, some crossed over the ceiling as if holding it up. Others were charred or rotted and lay across the ground where they had fallen.

"We're underground," Autumn marveled.

It was true. Before they had been simply under *snow*, but at some point, without even realizing it, Flurry had dug so deep that he'd gone underground, and his tunnel had emptied out into this vast earthen chamber. It seemed impossible, until Winter realized something.

"We're not in my Sparkledom anymore," she said. "I can feel it." She looked at Autumn. "Did we cross over to yours?"

"No," said Autumn. She and Winter both turned to Spring, but Spring was already shaking her head. "Nothing in my Sparkledom would look like this," she said. "Not even underground."

"So if we're not in my land," Winter said, "and we haven't crossed into either of yours, we have to be in..."

"The Barrens," Summer said.

# CHAPTER
# 4

**W**e have to turn back," Spring said. "Right now."

"You can't be serious," Winter replied.

"I can't?" Spring asked. She thought about it a minute, then decided, "Yes! I *can* be serious! We have to turn back! Now!"

Winter understood Spring's fear. The Barrens was no place for Sparkles. It was the home of Bluster Tempest and his Weeds. Their wide land circled the sisters' Sparkledoms. Nothing green grew in the Barrens. All the trees were old, dead, and thorny. Lightning, tornadoes, and earthquakes pummeled the land constantly. The storms popped up out of nowhere, igniting fires, throwing trees around like toys, and ripping open the earth.

Normally, Winter would have no desire to go to

the Barrens, but this was *not* a normal occasion. "We can't turn back. Flurry came this way. Look."

She pointed to the ground, where large circular paw prints led across the cavern. They disappeared where Flurry had climbed over or smashed through the wooden beams, then kept going until they turned a distant corner.

"We have to follow him," Winter said.

"Follow him?" Spring whined. "But that would take us farther into the Barrens!"

"Maybe we should think it over first," Autumn offered.

"Think *what* over?" Winter snapped. "Flurry's never been in the Barrens. He could get lost. He could get hurt. He could run into Bluster Tempest or one of the Weeds! You really want to think about what would happen then?"

"I don't," Summer said. "Let's go get him."

"Wait," Autumn said. "I have a better idea. Let's call Mother."

"Yes!" Spring said eagerly. "She'll know what to do."

"*I* know what to do," Winter said. "Besides, the call won't work. We're underground. There's no path to the sky."

Spring looked dejected. She knew Winter was right.

"Spring, you don't have to come if you don't want to," Summer said gently. "Neither do you, Autumn. It's okay."

Autumn shook her head. "I can't let the two of you go into the Barrens alone. I'll come too."

Summer and Winter smiled gratefully at Autumn. Then all three sisters turned to Spring. The youngest Sparkle scrunched her lips together and closed her eyes. When she opened them again, they were determined. "The only thing worse than going with the three of you into the most horrible place in the world is being away from you," she said. "I'm coming too."

Winter gave Spring a huge hug. Snowball even popped his head out of Winter's hood to lick Spring on the nose. Afterward, Winter pointed down to Flurry's trail. "We follow the paw prints. Flurry, here we come!"

She led her sisters through the cavern, which turned out to be far larger than just a single room. It was more like a mine that seemed to stretch on forever. The Sparkles followed the paw prints, but it wasn't easy. A few times their path was blocked by tall jumbles of fallen wooden beams. Summer barely noticed. She took running starts and easily leaped even the highest piles. Winter made it over them the same way she imagined Flurry had. She clambered hand over foot, trusting her snow gear to protect her from sharp edges. Spring and Autumn took their time picking their way across the obstacles, moving slowly so they didn't get splinters.

Winter would never admit it to her sisters, but she was getting a little tired. They had already walked a long way. Yet the minute she thought this, her heart started pounding with excitement. If *she* was tired walking this far, Flurry must have been *exhausted*. The walk was hard work, and he hated hard work. He'd much rather nap.

There was a corner up ahead, and Winter ran to reach it. Now that the image of Flurry napping was in her head, she couldn't get it out. She was positive that all she had to do was turn the corner and she'd find her bear curled against a wall, fast asleep.

Winter ran faster. She pictured herself wrapping her arms around Flurry, telling him how much she loved him and how sorry she was. She leaped around the corner, so excited to see Flurry that she didn't look where she was going. She ran as fast as she could, scanning the walls for a sign of her sleeping bear until—

"Winter, look out!" Summer shouted.

Winter stopped cold. She was inches away from a large, low wooden platform. In the middle of the platform sat a big hinge, plus a thick metal bar with angry-looking serrated edges.

"It's a giant mousetrap," Autumn said as she and Spring caught up to their sisters. "Mother said something about them once. Outworlders use them."

"To catch giant mice?" Spring asked. "That's so fun! Do they tame the giant mice and ride them all over the Outworld?"

Autumn didn't answer. She didn't want to upset Spring.

Cautiously, the sisters moved closer to the mousetrap. Winter noticed crumbs on it, the remnants of a snack. When something took the snack, that triggered the toothy metal bar, which snapped back onto the snack thief.

"Ooh, look at the fluff!" Spring said, pointing at the bar. Caught under it was a large puff of white fur. "It looks just like Flurry's!"

Her delighted smile faded as she realized what that meant. "Autumn," she asked worriedly, "the Outlanders don't use mousetraps to *tame* the giant mice, do they?"

"No," Autumn answered, "and the Weeds don't use them to tame bears. We're lucky it only got his fur."

"This place is way too dangerous for Flurry," Winter added. "We have to keep going and find him."

"We will," Summer said. "But stick together and keep an eye out for traps. If there's one, there's going to be more."

Summer was right. As the sisters followed the paw prints, turning and branching into tunnel after tunnel, room after room, they saw several more traps.

Yet just like the giant mousetrap, it seemed that Flurry had set them all off when he passed. In one corridor, for example, the sisters had to crawl under a giant wooden spike that stretched all the way across the room.

"Look," Summer said. She pointed to a network of cracks around the pointy end of the spike. "It shot out of that wall and slammed into this one."

"I bet this was the trigger," Winter said. She nodded to the floor beneath the spike. The letter *W* was scratched into the ground, marred by a large Flurry-print. "Flurry set it off when he stepped on the *W*."

"*W* for Weeds," Spring murmured. "Flytraps and frights, I'm glad Flurry ducked."

"And he taught us something," Summer noted.

"That bears can duck, but ducks can't bear?" Spring asked. "Oh wait, they *can* bear. They can bear water and bread crumbs and—"

"No," Summer interrupted. "He taught us we can't touch anything with a *W* on it."

The other Sparkles agreed, and as they kept following Flurry's path, they carefully avoided the scattered *W*s scratched into the floor. Each time they saw one, they glanced around and easily found the trap. A sack of bricks hung over one trigger, the outline of a trapdoor surrounded another.

"This one's strange," Summer said as she noticed yet another *W* on the ground up ahead. "I don't see any trap at all."

"Maybe Flurry already set it off," Autumn offered.

"Even if he did, we'd still see it," Winter said.

"I don't like hidden traps." Spring shuddered.

"Don't worry about it," Winter said. "If we avoid the trigger, we're fine."

But Spring *did* worry about it. She lagged behind her sisters, moving slowly and looking everywhere except at her feet. She'd feel much better if she could at least see the trap she was avoiding. Her eyes scanned the ceiling, the wall on the left, the wall on the right . . .

*CRUNCH.*

Spring froze. *Now* she looked down at her feet.

One purple sandal stood firmly on the letter *W*.

"Oh, no!" she yelped.

Winter, Summer, and Autumn turned to see Spring frozen in place, her eyes wide and scared, her foot on the trigger of something terrible. In a flash, Summer ran toward Spring, planted the bottom of her scepter on the ground, and hurled herself into the air. She smacked into Spring and knocked them both to the floor, several feet away from the *W*.

"Aw, Summer, I love you too!" Spring cooed. "But sometimes your hugs hurt!"

"I wasn't hugging you," she said. "I was getting you away from the trap."

"But there *is* no trap!" Spring said delightedly. "See?"

It was true. Nothing bad had happened since Spring stepped on the letter.

"Maybe the Weeds changed while they were building this tunnel," Spring enthused. "Maybe they decided to stop making traps and be nice."

"Weeds are *never* nice," Winter assured her. "The trap's probably broken. We got lucky."

The minute she said the words, a hissing sound filled the room.

"Snakes?" Autumn asked.

Spring shook her head. She knew snakes' hissing language and this wasn't it.

Then the stench hit. All four Sparkles clamped their hands over their noses.

"Ugh! What *is* that?" Summer choked.

"It's disgusting!" Autumn agreed.

"It's like someone pooped in my nose!" Winter said.

Spring shook her head. "Poop is nicer. It's natural. This is . . ."

"Horrible!" Summer gagged. "Ew, when I talk it gets in my mouth and I can *taste* it!"

In Winter's hood, even baby Snowball coughed and sputtered at the rotting stink.

"We've got to get out of here," Autumn said.

"Run!" Winter screamed.

The Sparkles raced forward, but the odor followed them. It clung to their clothes. Their eyes watered. They poured on the speed, desperate to get away.

When they rounded the next corner, Winter squinted. Far ahead at the top of a ramp, Winter saw a small stream of sunlight. Her heart leaped and she took a deep breath. Behind the hideous odor, she could already feel the deliciously fresh air.

"This way!" she cried. "Come on!"

The sisters raced toward the sunlight, so desperate to reach clean air that they didn't even see the large stretch of rope sprawled on the floor—or the *W* carved into the ground beneath it.

They didn't see it, but Autumn stepped on it.

Instantly, the rope snapped upward, catching all four Sparkles in what was now a large net suspended from the ceiling. The Sparkles screamed as they tumbled into one another, crunched and tangled together at the bottom of the pouch.

"What's happening?" Spring wailed.

"What do you think's happening?" Winter asked. "We're trapped!"

"I know that," Spring cried, "but we're *moving*!"

The Sparkles stopped struggling and looked up. A panel had opened in the ceiling. It revealed a long, dark hole, and their entire net prison was rising straight toward it.

## CHAPTER
## 5

The Sparkles couldn't see a thing.

Once they passed through the hole in the cavern's ceiling, it slid shut again. Without the hole, there was no light at all.

The sisters didn't speak. Instead they listened for clues that might tell them where they were. There weren't many. They heard the creak of whatever pulleys were drawing them higher and higher. They felt a damp chill. They smelled wet moss.

Where were they?

What would happen when they stopped?

Would the Weeds be waiting?

With a loud mechanical screech, the net stopped rising and instead swung lazily back and forth. Normally Winter liked to swing, but not when she was on the bottom of a sack all tangled in her sisters' limbs.

She strained her senses but saw the same thing whether her eyes were open or closed. Her ears didn't pick up anything beyond her and her sisters' nervously measured breaths.

"I think we're alone," Winter finally said.

"Alone and stuck," Summer agreed. "Think you could move your knee? My arm's going numb."

"I can't *feel* my knee. Someone's lying on it."

"Can we shift just a little? There's an elbow in the middle of my back."

"Ow-ow-ow. My arm doesn't bend that way."

"Do you think we'll stop swinging soon?" Autumn asked. "I feel a little woozy."

"No," Winter said. "No way are you getting sick in this thing. Not acceptable."

"Then I'd suggest we get out," Autumn said. "Or at least stop moving."

"On it," Summer said. "I'll burn a hole in the net."

She twisted and squirmed, accidentally kicking and elbowing the other Sparkles.

"I can't." Summer sighed. "My scepter's stuck. How about you, Winter? Maybe if you ice the rope, we can break it."

"I'm all pretzeled up," Winter said. "I can't even reach my own nose."

"Does it itch?" Spring asked. "I could ask Snowball to scratch it."

Guilt washed over Winter. She had forgotten all about the baby fox. "Is he okay?" she asked.

A low coo came from her hood. Spring giggled. "He's fine. A little squished, but he says that just makes him cozier. He also says he'd be happy to scratch your nose, but he's worried he might hurt you. His claws are awfully sharp."

"*How* sharp?" Winter asked. "Sharp enough to cut a hole in this rope?"

More fox noises came from inside Winter's hood.

"He thinks so," Spring said. "Should he try?"

"YES!" Winter said.

"Wait," Autumn interrupted. "We don't know how high up we are. What if he cuts a hole and we fall so far we get hurt?"

"That would be bad," Winter admitted, "but it would also be bad hanging here all smushed together until we starve to death."

"Or have to use the bathroom," Spring noted.

"Also not acceptable," Winter said.

"I'm not saying we stay here," Autumn said, "but maybe Snowball should find out about the room before he cuts us down. Can't foxes see in the dark?"

"What do you think, Snowball?" Spring asked. "Can you see in here?"

Winter felt a tickle as the pup crawled out of her hood and perched on top of her head. "Ow!" She winced. "Those little claws *are* sharp."

Snowball yipped happily, growled a little, yapped several times, then howled.

"He says sorry for scratching you," Spring said. "He also says we're in a small stone room with round walls, like the inside of a tower. The net is hanging from a hook in the ceiling, but we're only a few feet off the floor. We might get bruised if we fall, but we won't get badly hurt. Oh, and Winter, he also wants to know if you have any more candy canes."

"Tons," Winter answered Snowball. "Get us out of this net and they're all yours."

The pup yipped again, then hopped off Winter's head. The Sparkles felt him work his way around the net, then heard little growls and scratches as his teeth and claws worked the rope fibers. How long would it be until Snowball cut enough rope that they'd fall free? They had no idea.

"AAAAHHH!"

With no warning, the net fell open and the Sparkles tumbled to the ground. Winter sprung back up immediately. She stretched her limbs as far as they could go, thrilled to have space.

"Snowball, you are the best!" she shouted. "If I could see you, I would kiss you!"

Winter fell back as a small ball of fur hurled itself

at her face. She wrapped her arms around Snowball and kissed him square on the snout.

"And don't think I forgot," she said. She pulled a candy cane from her pocket and peeled off the wrapper. Snowball grabbed it and hopped back into Winter's hood to enjoy the treat. Winter grinned, but then she thought of Flurry and how jealous he'd be if he saw her kissing Snowball. And worse, giving Snowball one of his candy canes. In her head, Winter could even hear his outraged cries.

*"HOOOOOOWWWWWLLLL!"*

Winter gasped. That howl wasn't in her head at all! It was coming from somewhere outside the room! "Flurry!" she cried. She ran forward in the darkness, her hands outstretched until they found the wall. She beat on it with her fists. "Flurry! I'm here! Can you hear me?"

He howled again. It sounded faint and far away, but it was him!

"What is he saying, Spring?" Winter asked. "Can he hear me?"

"I'm sorry, Winter," Spring said, "but you know I can't understand Flurry."

Of course Winter knew that. She was just so eager to hear from her bear that she hadn't thought about it. Spring could speak with almost any animal, but not with her sisters' special pets. Shade the jaguar, Whisper the elephant, and Flurry were so bonded to Summer, Autumn, and Winter that they had their own communication. They couldn't exactly chat like Spring and her unicorn, Dewdrop, but the pairs understood each other just as perfectly.

*Almost* as perfectly. These howls were a complete mystery to Winter, and they were making her crazy.

"He sounds like he's hurt!" she wailed. "We have to help him!"

"We will," Autumn said soothingly. "And I have an idea. I just need to see how the wall feels."

"Pansies and pinecones, you speak Wall?" Spring gasped.

"She means she's *feeling* the wall," Summer said. "With her hands. To look for weak spots. Right?"

"Exactly," Autumn said. "And I think I found one. Stand back."

The sisters retreated as far from the sound of

Autumn's voice as they could go. Then Autumn chanted:

"I feel weakness in this wall,
so let my wind now make it fall!"

Orange sparkles lit up the room as Autumn waved her scepter over her head, around and around. In the glow, the sisters saw their prison for the first time. It was just as Snowball had described it, round and small. The tattered net still hung from its hook in the center of the room, but now it whipped and swayed in the wild gust Autumn was creating. She swirled the wind faster and faster until it was a tiny hurricane. Then, just when it seemed too powerful for her to control, she flicked her arm and hurled the storm forward.

Autumn's wind slammed into the wall's weak spot with so much force that it blasted open a Sparkle-sized hole. Light spilled into the room. Autumn turned to her sisters and smiled at them. Tears filled her eyes.

"Autumn, you're crying!" Spring said. "What's wrong?"

"It's just so good to see the three of you!" Autumn said.

"But we've been together this whole time!" Winter said.

"Yeah, but it was dark." Summer smiled. "I think she means it's good to actually *see* us."

Autumn nodded.

"We love you too, Autumn," Summer said. "You did a great job."

She and Spring ran to Autumn for a huge hug.

"You are hopelessly sentimental," Winter said. "But it's good to see you too." She joined her sisters in the hug, but they jumped apart when Flurry howled again.

It was *not* a happy howl.

They pushed their way through the hole in the wall and ran toward the sound of his voice. Winter could only hope they weren't too late.

## CHAPTER
# 6

The Sparkles were running through some kind of castle. It was enormous, but it was in bad shape. Dirty clothes covered every surface. Winter had to leap midstride to avoid a pile of Weed underwear, which is something she *never* wanted to see.

"Where there's Weed underwear, there are Weeds," Summer said. "Keep an eye out."

"Do I have to?" Spring asked. "If they're not wearing their underwear, they're *naked* Weeds!"

"*Ewww!*" wailed the Sparkles.

As they zoomed through room after room following Flurry's howls, Winter noticed filthy footprints everywhere. They covered the floors, every piece of furniture, the walls, and even the ceiling. Winter was all for playing on every possible surface, but at least she cleaned up after herself. Sure, she had magical help, but the Weeds had magic too. There was no excuse.

"Ew-ew-ew-ew-ew," Spring yelped as they ran. "Dirty Weed clothes touching my feet!"

"It smells almost as bad as the stink trap in the cavern," Summer muttered.

Actually, Winter thought it smelled worse. The castle's odor was a mix of mold, sweat, and rotten food. Not surprising, since mixed in with all the dirty laundry were half-filled candy wrappers, discarded pizza crusts, and ant-covered fuzzy somethings that might once have been cupcakes or brownies.

"How do they live like this?" Autumn asked.

"Stinkily," Spring answered.

Another Flurry howl made the girls run faster until finally they came to a massive set of wooden doors. They were slightly open, and when Flurry wailed once more it was clear he was right inside.

"Flurry!" Winter shouted. "We're here!"

Before she opened the door, she took a deep breath and prepared herself. These were the Weeds she was dealing with. They were capable of anything.

One more deep breath, then she burst into the room, scepter raised and ready for battle.

Her jaw dropped.

Winter thought she was ready for anything, but nothing could have prepared her for this.

The room was enormous, its high ceilings painted with images of snarling beasts. In its center stood a giant, splintery wooden table covered in platters piled high with food . . . and with Thunderbolt, one of the Four Weeds. He stood right on top of the table, one naked foot in a bowl of mashed potatoes and the other in a blueberry pie. He twanged an off-key guitar electrified by his own Weedy powers. His purple spiked hair bounced back and forth as he banged his head to the ear-splitting noise.

Flurry stood on his hind legs right in front of Thunderbolt. Quake, a short, squat Weed with hair that grew in butchered patches, boogied on the bear's head.

No wonder Flurry was howling. Between the screeching music and the Weed on his head, he must have been in terrible pain!

At least that's what Winter thought. Then she realized Flurry was smiling.

And shimmying.

And shaking his behind.

"Whoa! Whoa! Whoa!" Winter hollered. "Are you *dancing*?"

No one heard her. The music was too loud. Winter stormed to the table, ready to tackle Thunderbolt and rip the guitar out of his hands.

"Winter, don't," Autumn said. "Electrified."

She was right. Touching Thunderbolt while he worked the guitar wouldn't be a good plan. Instead Winter grabbed a cornbread muffin and threw it in his face.

"Ow!"

Thunderbolt stopped playing, so Flurry and Quake stopped dancing.

"What happened?" Quake complained. "Where's the music?"

"Ask the Sparkles," Thunderbolt retorted. "Comin'

in here and ruining everything. Who invited you, anyway?"

Winter's mouth dropped open. For a minute she couldn't even find the words.

"Who...wha...who *invited* us?" she finally spluttered. "Nobody invited us! We risked our lives to come and save Flurry!"

"Save him from what?" Quake asked.

"From...from..." Winter looked around again at the food, the guitar, and the disappointed looks on Quake's and Flurry's faces.

"Um, Winter?" Summer said. "It looks like we saved him from a party."

"No, that can't be right. I heard you crying," she told Flurry, "like you were hurt."

"He was hungry," Quake said. He clicked his tongue and Flurry obediently plucked Quake off his head and set him on the table next to Thunderbolt. Quake sat on a large roasted chicken as if it were a stool.

"Aw, that's nice," Quake said. "Feels warm. Thanks, Butch."

The bear saluted in response.

"*Butch?*" Winter blurted. "His name is *Flurry!*"

"Flurry's too girly," Quake said. "Butch suits him better. Don't it, Butch?"

Flurry howled—the same awful, painful howl the Sparkles had heard before.

"It doesn't sound like he enjoys that name," Spring said.

"It ain't the name," Quake said. "I told ya, Butchie needs food. Here ya go, Butchie-Bear."

"*Butchie-Bear?*" Winter repeated.

Quake picked up a giant bowl of cornbread muffins. Flurry opened wide.

"You can't give him all that!" Winter exploded.

"You're right," Quake said. "I forgot the honey!" He moved across the table, stepping in seven different side dishes, then grabbed a squeeze bottle of honey and emptied it over the muffins. "*Now* we're ready. Eat 'em up!"

Quake tossed the honey-coated muffins out of the bowl, and Flurry swallowed them in a single gulp.

"Now look what you did!" Winter wailed. "He's going to get a bellyache!"

"Winter, I've seen you give him ten candy canes at a time," Summer said.

"That's different," Winter said. "And whose side are you on?"

"Thunderbolt's standing in potatoes and pie, and Quake used a cooked chicken as a butt-warmer," Summer said. "Of course I'm on your side. I'm just saying, Flurry doesn't look like his belly's upset."

It was true. Winter didn't want to believe it, but Flurry looked very happy hanging out with Quake and Thunderbolt. As for his belly, Flurry was already howling for more.

"See?" Quake said. "He's *still* hungry. Hey, Thunderbolt, move your foot."

Thunderbolt shook his feet around inside the food platters. Mashed potatoes and pie filling splattered everywhere. The Sparkles dodged to avoid the spatter, but a large splotch of blueberry goo smacked onto Spring's skirt.

"Cacti and cauliflower!" Spring wailed. Then she studied the stain and smiled. "But it's in the shape of Dewdrop! Thank you, Thunderbolt!"

"Uh, you're welcome?" the Weed replied.

"Hey," Quake called to him, "when I said move your foot, I meant get it out of the pie!"

"Oh. Sure." Thunderbolt lifted his foot. It was covered in blueberry goop. He stared at it for a

minute, then sat down and pulled the foot toward his mouth.

"No," Autumn said to him. "I can't handle it. You cannot *possibly* . . ."

He could. Thunderbolt leaned forward and ran his tongue from his heel to his toes, lapping up the blueberry filling. Then he slipped his tongue between his toes.

"I'm going to try very hard to convince myself I didn't see that," Autumn said, "so maybe one day I can eat again. If anyone needs me for anything, just shake me." She touched her middle fingers to her thumbs and closed her eyes.

Quake, meanwhile, held the mutilated blueberry pie toward Flurry. "Here ya go, Butchie. You like pie, right?"

Flurry whined hungrily.

"You can't eat that pie!" Winter shouted to her bear. "There was foot in that pie! That is *foot pie!*"

"Man, Butch, you were right," Thunderbolt said between toe licks. "She's no fun at all. No wonder you moved to the Barrens."

"Flurry did not move to the Barrens!" Winter objected. "And he definitely didn't say I'm not fun! I'm a *lot* of fun!"

"Prove it," Thunderbolt said. He held out his foot. "There's a little pie left underneath the pinkie toe. Eat it."

"That's not fun, that's *disgusting*!" Winter yelled. "And how would either of you Weeds know anything Flurry said? You speak Bear now?"

"Tell her what you told us, Butch," Thunderbolt suggested.

Flurry obeyed. He acted out everything that had happened in the fort. He crouched low and pretended to be Winter discovering Snowball, cooing over the pantomimed animal and cuddling it in his arms. Then he took a step back and became himself trying to get Winter's attention. He turned and became Winter again, putting his paws on his hips. He waved a scolding claw, then pointed angrily, like Winter sending Flurry away. Miming his own response, Flurry got down on all fours and slinked sadly away. When he finished he stood tall, crossed his arms, and put his snout in the air, daring Winter to deny it.

"You see?" Thunderbolt said. "You didn't want him, so he doesn't want you."

Winter ignored him. Flurry's show broke her heart. She knew she'd hurt his feelings but had no idea how badly until she saw it through his eyes. She moved to Flurry and took the big bear's paw.

"I'm so sorry, Flurry," she said. "I shouldn't have yelled at you, and I didn't mean to ignore you. I know I paid a lot of attention to the puppy, but that never changed how I feel about you. I love you. Will you please come home with me?"

Flurry didn't say anything, and Winter worried he wouldn't forgive her. Then he squeezed her into the tightest hug ever, dropped to all fours so they were nose-to-snout, and licked her face.

"That's it, Butchie! Taste her!" Thunderbolt cheered.

"Bet you're scared now," Quake chided. "If you're not careful, our bear's gonna eat you up!"

"I think I have something he'd rather eat up,"

Winter said. She reached into her pocket and pulled out a candy cane.

"Didn't she just complain that the Weeds were giving him too much food?" Summer asked.

"Yes," Autumn agreed, "but they're having a moment. We should let it go."

The smell of peppermint filled the room as Winter unwrapped the candy, but she had forgotten she'd promised the candy canes in her pocket to someone else. Once the scent tickled his nose, Snowball bounded excitedly out of Winter's hood, ran down her arm, and grabbed the candy cane in his mouth.

Flurry reared back, shocked and angry.

"Um, Snowball"—Winter winced—"that candy cane was actually for Flurry."

Snowball didn't understand, and his desire to help with Flurry was apparently eclipsed by his desire for candy. He took his treat and trotted back into Winter's hood.

Winter looked into Flurry's stormy eyes and scrambled for an explanation. "Okay, yes, I have the baby fox with me," she said, "and yes, I gave him some of your candy canes, but it does *not* mean I'm replacing you! Would I really follow you all the way into the Barrens if I didn't love you?"

Flurry thought about it a moment, and Winter felt a glimmer of hope. Then the bear stuck his nose in the platter of mashed potatoes, snorted them deep, and blew them at Winter as hard as he could. Gooey potato coated the Sparkle's face.

"Way to go, Butchie!" Quake cheered.

"Atta boy!" Thunderbolt added.

"Tubers and tiger's tails!" Spring gasped. "I can't believe he did that!"

"Flurry has *definitely* spent too much time with the Weeds," Summer said.

The two boys scratched Flurry's back to congratulate him. Their dirty hands left smudges on the bear's white fur, but he didn't look like he minded. In fact, he looked proud of himself.

Winter understood. Flurry wanted her to know that *he* could make new friends too. She cleared swaths of potato goo from her eyes, nose, and mouth, and tried not to think about the fact that they'd been both in Flurry's nose and stomped by Thunderbolt's filthy feet.

"Okay, I guess I deserved that," she told Flurry. "Now can you come home?"

"Butchie's home is in the Barrens," Thunderbolt said.

"Yeah, with us!" Quake agreed.

"Me and Quake, we know a thing or two about loyalty," Thunderbolt told Flurry. "We won't dump you for somethin' little and cute."

"I did not dump you for something little and cute," Winter said to Flurry . . . just as Snowball crawled back out of her hood to lick the remaining mashed potatoes off her face.

Flurry glowered, then turned his back on Winter and raced away on all fours.

"Flurry, wait!" Winter cried. "Stop!"

He didn't stop. He galloped alongside the wooden table as Quake and Thunderbolt ran on top of it.

"Wait for us, Butchie!" Thunderbolt crowed.

"Yeah, we wanna come!" Quake yelled.

The boys paid no attention to the platters of food

in their path. They knocked over gravy, stomped into spaghetti, and slipped and slid through a pile of green jelly.

Autumn drew her scepter and turned to Winter. "Should I stop Flurry?" she asked. "I could try to make a wind that would blow him back to us."

Winter shook her head. "I want him to come home because he *wants* to, not because we made him."

She watched sadly as Flurry rounded the far end of the table, then winced as Quake and Thunderbolt leaped off its top to smack down hard on Flurry's back.

"Let's bust out of this place, Butchie!" hollered Thunderbolt. "Full speed ahead!" He tugged on Flurry's neck and steered him straight toward the wall. Winter couldn't believe it. "Flurry, slow down!" she cried.

"Butchie don't take orders from you no more," Quake hollered. "You want to order somethin' around, try your little fox!"

That got to Flurry. He set his jaw, lowered his

head, and thundered straight ahead. Winter couldn't look. She cringed away, but heard a terrible splintering *CRACK*. When she peeked back up, there was a bear-shaped hole in the thick wooden wall.

"Flurry!" she cried. She and her sisters raced to the jagged, splintered gap, but Flurry was already far gone, galloping through the Barrens with Quake and Thunderbolt whooping joyfully on his back.

"Winter?" Spring asked worriedly. "What do we do now?"

Before Winter could answer, Thunderbolt spun around and pointed his wand at them. They didn't hear what he shouted, but an instant later a bolt of lightning hit a *W* scratched into the wall next to them. The floor under the Sparkles' feet fell away, and Autumn, Winter, Spring, and Summer tumbled down into darkness.

# CHAPTER
# 7

The four Sparkles whooshed down a long, twisting tunnel. They couldn't see a thing, and all they could hear was the sound of their own screams. After what seemed like forever, a door at the end of the slide creaked open. They tumbled outside and splashed into murky water. Winter sank into its depths but quickly kicked her way to the surface, where she treaded water next to her sisters.

"Everyone okay?" Summer asked.

"I'm good," Spring said.

"I'm okay," Autumn agreed.

Winter didn't answer. She was scoping out the situation. They'd been spit into a moat, right next to the steep castle wall. The wall was polished so smooth that Winter knew not even she could climb

it. She *could* get back into the castle by climbing up the slide—she climbed up a slide to get into her bed every night—but the door that had opened to eject the Sparkles had already slid shut.

"I looked too," Summer said. "The other side's just as bad." She pointed to the far bank. Not only was it a long distance away, but it was also covered in thorny vines.

"Is this a bad time to mention I'm not very good in the water?" Autumn asked. She splashed clumsily, and Summer arranged herself so she could help her sister and keep them both afloat.

Unlike her sisters, Spring didn't seem concerned about their situation. She floated easily on her back and gazed up at the sky until she heard a happy yip.

"Snowball!" she cried as the pup splashed through the water. She giggled as he climbed onto her chest, shook himself dry, then curled into a ball and settled in for a nap. "Awwww, look! He's using me like a little float!"

"That's it!" Winter cried. "Spring, speaking of floats..."

"Yes! It's so funny we're speaking of floats, because I was just looking up at the clouds . . . Did you notice that all the clouds in the Barrens are storm clouds? Which I thought would make me really sad, but storm clouds can be pretty too. Like that one—it looks just like a root beer float!"

"Not *drinking* floats, Spring," Winter said. "We need a float to *float* on. Those plants on the far shore—can you use them?"

"Yes!" Spring said. "That's a great idea!" Without disturbing Snowball, she pulled out her scepter and recited:

"Thorns, grow soft and weave a path,
so we can leave this murky bath!"

She waved her scepter, then pointed it across the moat. Purple sparkles danced out of her scepter orb and soared into the thorny vines. A broad strip of sparkle-covered vines knit themselves together and grew into a wide woven path that quickly arced across the water.

"Spring, you're a lifesaver," Summer said. She pulled Autumn to the bridge and the two of them held on as they caught their breath. Winter was about to join them, but then she noticed something bubbling in the water. The bubbles burst to the surface far beyond where Spring and Snowball floated lazily along. They were so far away, Winter almost ignored them.

But then they moved nearer.

Winter told herself not to worry. The water was disgusting. It was probably swamp gas bubbling to the surface.

Except swamp gas didn't move.

Something was coming toward them.

Whatever it was, Winter didn't want to shout and get its attention, so she quickly swam to her littlest sister's side and whispered to her urgently.

"Spring, hurry," Winter said. "We need to get onto that bridge you made right now."

Spring gasped. "It *is* a bridge! And you asked for a float! I'm sorry, Winter. Are you upset?"

The bubbles were much closer now. And they were speeding up.

"No!" Winter assured her. "A bridge is perfect. But we need to use it. *Now!*"

"You seem upset," Spring said. "Are you sure everything's okay?"

Snowball was the one who answered. He must have sensed whatever was coming, because he jumped to his feet and the fur on his back rose. He growled low, then barked angrily.

Spring looked at him, wide-eyed. "There's a *monster* behind us?"

"And it's charging!" Winter screamed. The bubbles were zooming toward them now. "Summer, Autumn," she called, "get on the bridge! And Spring, *swim!*"

Summer hoisted herself onto the bridge with a single push, then pulled Autumn up after her. Spring, meanwhile, flipped onto her stomach, placed Snowball between her shoulder blades, and crawl-stroked as fast as she could. Winter tried to keep up, but she couldn't stop peeking over her shoulder. The bubbles were *very* close now. The Sparkles were running out of time.

"Hurry!" Winter cried.

She got to the bridge moments after Spring. She boosted her littlest sister out of the water, then lunged onto the bridge herself. She collapsed onto it just a second before the bubbles hit the side of the bridge, disappeared, then gurgled again on the other side.

"It's okay." Winter panted. "We're safe."

"Unless it can jump," Summer said.

The four sisters and the fox looked at one another for a moment. Then Winter scooped up Snowball and wailed, "RUN!"

The girls poured every bit of energy into their tired legs, but they were a long way from shore. Winter peeked over her shoulder, then wished she hadn't. The monster's bubble trail raced alongside them so quickly it looked like a speedboat wake.

"Run faster!" Winter screamed.

They did, but Winter knew they couldn't keep it up for long. Her own breath rasped in her throat as she pushed herself to her limit. Finally, just when she thought she might collapse, they neared the other side of the bridge. Winter relaxed a little, confident that everything would be okay.

Then the most hideous creature she had ever seen leaped out of the water and landed on the bridge between the Sparkles and the shore. Winter, Spring, Summer, Autumn, and even Snowball screamed. The creature roared.

The beast was twice as long as Winter's biggest sleigh. Its body was thick, scaly, green, and snakelike, but with a huge, veiny blue tail and front flippers. Its face held fishy eyes that were blank and evil, and a mouth that gaped open to reveal three sets of sharp teeth.

"Run the other way!" Winter hollered.

The Sparkles turned and raced for the castle. It was a dead end, but what else could they do?

*GALUMPH! GALUMPH! GALUMPH!*

Winter didn't dare look over her shoulder. She knew what she would see. The creature was following them. It was pulling itself along the bridge with those front flippers and slapping its snaky body after them.

She couldn't help it. She had to peek.

What she saw stopped her in her tracks.

The monster was galumphing after them, but only three of them were running.

Spring had stopped. She stood in the middle of the bridge, looking up at the monster curiously.

"*Spring!*" Winter shrieked. "What are you doing?"

Her yell made Summer and Autumn stop and turn too. Neither liked what they saw.

"Spring," Autumn said gently, "I think you should come with us."

"I don't think so," Spring said. "I think I should try to talk to it."

"*What?*" Winter exploded.

"Spring," Summer said, "that's not an animal. It's a monster. We need to get *away* from it."

Spring looked back at her sisters. "Where will we go?"

They didn't answer. They didn't have an answer. Their only options were the polished castle wall or the water. Neither offered escape. Winter pulled out her scepter. "Then we'll fight."

Summer and Autumn clearly agreed. They pulled out their scepters as well.

"Let me try first," Spring said. "Please."

There was something about the way Spring said

"please." It wasn't like she was asking her sisters, she was *telling* them this was something she needed to do.

"Okay," Autumn said. But she, Winter, and Summer kept their scepters out, just in case.

Spring turned back to the monster. She walked toward it, a huge smile on her face.

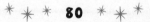

The monster didn't seem impressed. It seemed hungry. It pulled itself even faster along the bridge.

"Hi!" Spring waved.

The monster didn't respond. It was right in front of Spring now. It reared up on its snaky body and opened its mouth wide, ready to chomp down with its rows of teeth.

"Ready?" Winter counted down the seconds until she, Summer, and Autumn would attack. "Three . . . two . . ."

"I love you," Spring said.

The monster froze. It made a noise that sounded like *Huh?*

"I mean, I know I don't really know you, so maybe you think I can't possibly love you, but I do. I've never seen anyone like you. I mean, I've seen a fish and a snake and a shark and a whale, and you're a little like all of those, but different. It's like all those little creatures were smushed up and thrown together and shaken up, and you came out!"

Spring thought a moment, then frowned. "Except not quite like that because smushing up little creatures is mean and yucky."

The monster lowered back down to its front flippers. Its teeth were still bared, but it looked . . . interested.

"I can tell you want to eat us," Spring said. "My sisters want to fight you. They have powers. They're pretty strong. I think you might be stronger and would end up having us for lunch, but you'd get hurt on the way, and that would make me sad. If it's okay with you, I'd rather talk. Then afterward, if you still want to eat us, I understand."

There was no response from the monster. It simply stared down at Spring as if sizing her up . . . or imagining how she'd taste.

"What do you think is happening?" Summer whispered.

"I'm not sure," Autumn admitted.

"Me neither," Winter said, "but I'm ready to hit that beast with everything we've got."

The creature was still for another moment, then quickly rolled onto its back. It squeaked and groaned with a voice that sounded like an upset stomach. Life poured into its eyes, and it gestured wildly with its flippers.

"Really?" Spring responded. "No . . . You don't say . . . They *did* that to you? . . . Well, no wonder! I'd feel the same way!"

As her sisters looked on with open mouths, Spring plopped down next to the beast and started rubbing its belly. When it got overly anxious, she comforted it with soothing words. "No, no, you can forget all about that now. Things will be different, I promise."

"Unbelievable," Winter said.

"Or kind of very believable." Summer smiled.

"My thoughts exactly," Autumn said.

The three Sparkles put their scepters away and joined Spring. "So, um, we're all friends now?" Winter asked.

Spring nodded. "He only wanted to eat us because he's starving. The Weeds never feed him. He lives on moat muck and anything that falls in from the castle. The boys never clean the water either, which I guess works since they don't feed him and at least this way he has the muck, but Sammy's awfully uncomfortable and unhappy."

"Sammy?" Winter asked.

"That's his name. It's different in his language. More like"—Spring threw back her head and gurgle-cried like a yodeling whale—"but Sammy's easier to say. And he likes it. Right, Sammy?"

The monster clapped his fins together.

"I told him he could come live in my lagoon," Spring said. "He'll be much happier there."

"That's very kind of you," Autumn said, "but how will we get him to the lagoon?"

"Show them how we'll get you to my Sparkledom, Sammy!" Spring said.

Sammy rolled back onto his feet and squeezed his fishy eyes in concentration. Two huge patches of scaly snake skin burst into thick, fluffy violet feathers.

"They're beautiful." Autumn gasped.

"Mm-hm." Spring rubbed her cheek against the feathers. "Soft, too. And look. Go ahead, Sammy."

Sammy unfolded the feathered layers to reveal giant wings. They looked so plush that Winter almost wanted to run to Sammy and cuddle in. Almost.

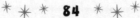

"I don't understand this at all," Summer said. "If he has wings, why hasn't he left the Barrens already?"

"Look closely," Spring said. "The Weeds clip him."

The Sparkles moved closer. Sammy's wings were so full and beautiful, it was hard to tell at first, but now Winter saw it. The feathers at the ends were ragged and tattered. Some looked so jagged they seemed more torn than clipped. Winter's stomach turned, and not just for Sammy. If this was how the Weeds treated animals, what would they do to Flurry?

"But, Spring, if his wings are too clipped to fly . . ." Suddenly, Autumn smiled as she realized what Spring was going to do.

"Just like the bridge!" Spring said. She took out her scepter and waved it at the thorny vines on the shore.

> "Fix what the Weeds have broke,
> so Sammy here can leave this
> moat!"

Purple sparkles streamed out from her scepter and coated the vines. Again, they wove together, but this time they shaped themselves into what looked like giant finger-gloves. Winter lost count of how many fingers were on each glove, and it was strange to her that all the fingers were different sizes. Yet when the vine snaked the gloves into place on Sammy's wings, the effect was magical. Spring's Sparkle Powers had filled in every spot the Weeds had shorn away. His new wing tips weren't the same fluffy violet as his natural feathers, but in their own way they were just as beautiful. Sammy's fishy face glowed with pride as he spread them wide.

Autumn wrapped Spring in a huge hug. "I am so proud to be your sister," she said.

"Really?" Spring's smile spread across her face. "Thank you, Autumn!"

"The patches are pretty amazing," Summer agreed, "but will they work?"

Sammy gurgled and groaned.

"They feel as good as his real ones," Spring

translated. "So now we can all get on his back and he'll fly us to his new home!"

"*Or*," Winter suggested, "he could fly us around the Barrens to find Flurry."

The other Sparkles looked sadly at one another.

"What?" Winter asked. "That's a great plan."

Autumn took Winter's hand. "If you really want to go after him, we will."

"Great, let's go then," Winter said. She walked toward Sammy, but Autumn still held her hand, so Winter didn't get very far. "Autumn, you have a strong grip."

"I'd just like you to think about it first," Autumn said. "Flurry *chose* to go with the Weeds. When we found him, he left us."

"So what are you saying?" Winter asked. "We just give up on him?"

"No, not at all," Autumn assured her. "I'm only saying maybe the best thing is to go home and wait. When he wants to come back to you, he will."

Winter thought about it. She hated the idea of leaving the Barrens without Flurry, but she also knew she couldn't force him home if he'd rather be here. Still, what if he *did* want to come home? What if all he needed was another apology?

As if sensing her worry, her sisters moved closer. Summer took Winter's other hand. Spring moved behind Winter and rested her head on Winter's shoulder. Snowball scurried out of Winter's hood and curled up on her head. Even Sammy looked sad for Winter.

Flurry wouldn't find this kind of love in the Barrens. He was upset, but he *must* want to come home. How could he not? When they were in Winter's Sparkledom, they had everything a Sparkle and a bear needed to be perfectly happy. Most of all, they had each other.

Suddenly, Winter knew. "Flurry's going to come home," she said. "I can feel it. He'll come home, and if I'm not there to see him and hug him and talk to him, he might not stay. I know it sounds crazy, and there's no way I can know that, but I *do*."

"It doesn't sound crazy," Autumn said. "It sounds like intuition. It's your heart telling you what it knows is true."

"And if your heart says you should get home, we should listen," Spring said.

Winter grinned and turned to Summer. "And if my heart says that I can get onto Sammy's back faster than you?"

"It's lying," Summer retorted.

The two raced to Sammy and leaped onto him at the exact same moment. Spring and Autumn took a bit longer to clamber up his scales, but soon all four Sparkles were looking at the world from Sammy's high snaky back.

"Take us to Winter's Sparkledom, please, Sammy!" Spring cried. "And hurry!"

# CHAPTER
# 8

**F**lurry had a headache. It wasn't awful, but running through a wall was hard on a bear's skull, and he'd been racing around with the two Weeds on his back ever since. He needed a nap. He slowed down and looked for a tree to curl up against, but the Weeds screamed and pressed their heels into his side. They said, "Go, Butchie!" and "Keep running, Butchie!"

Flurry didn't really understand. He always understood Winter, but anyone else's speech was a jumbled mystery mixed with a few recognizable words. Still, he could tell "Butchie" was what these boys called him. He also figured the heel-nudging meant they wanted him to go faster.

So he did. It was better, actually. It got him farther from Winter, and that's what Flurry wanted. Winter might have acted like she loved him, but it was pretty clear to Flurry that she loved the little fox more. Why else would she feed the fox his candy canes? So if Winter didn't love Flurry anymore, he wouldn't love her anymore either. Besides, he had these boys now. He didn't need anyone else.

Flurry ran for what seemed like hours, but then he slowed down again. It was definitely naptime. The boys still nudged and yelled, but Flurry figured they didn't understand how tired he was. He'd just have to show them. He stood on his hind legs so the boys slid off his back. He yawned and stretched.

"Hey!" the boy called Thunderbolt yelled. "What do you think you're doing?"

"I guess he's tired," said the boy named Quake.

"*I'm* not tired," Thunderbolt complained. "I wanna keep playing."

While Quake and Thunderbolt said words back and forth, Flurry looked for a napping spot. At home he'd curl up by the fire or in a cozy snowbank. Here the ground was hard-packed dirt with thorny roots sticking up in all directions. Every time he tried to lie down, he got poked. Finally, he saw tall grass. *That* would be comfortable. He lumbered toward the grass and curled up, but yelped immediately and jumped to his feet. The ground felt wet and muddy! He looked down at his side and saw he was streaked with thick stripes of muck.

"Hey, look!" Quake laughed. "He's a zebra!"

"Not yet, he's not," said Thunderbolt. He took a handful of mud and striped Flurry's other side, crowing, *"That's* a zebra."

The boys laughed. Now both of Flurry's sides felt dirty and wet.

"Come on, Butchie," Quake said. "You had a rest. Let's go play some more!"

The two boys climbed back onto Flurry and pressed their heels into his sides, but Flurry was still tired. Plus his belly hurt. All the pies and muffins had been delicious, but it was just too much.

Winter never would have let him eat that much.

She wouldn't have put mud on him.

She always let him nap when he needed to rest.

He missed her. He wanted to go back home. But

how could he? Winter had a new best friend now. She didn't want him around.

Then again...she had followed him to the Barrens. Maybe she did still love him?

Flurry winced as he remembered shooting mashed potatoes at her. That wasn't nice. It also wasn't nice to growl and run away. Even if Winter had loved him when she came to the Barrens, she wouldn't love him anymore.

The Weeds were his only friends now, so Flurry had to do what they wanted. He ran them around for a while. Then they hopped down and shouted words, but they also demonstrated things with their hands and bodies so Flurry understood. They wanted to play games. They had Flurry hop over branches that Thunderbolt shot down from the trees. Then Quake shook the earth and opened big holes in the ground for Flurry to leap. Next they goaded Flurry up a tree, then made him dance for candy.

The games weren't bad. At another time Flurry would have liked them all. But right now he was so tired and grumbly bellied that he couldn't even enjoy the candy. Flurry and Winter played hard all the time, but they also cuddled. She scratched behind his ears and lay on him and told him stories she made up just for him. He and Winter had fun, but they also loved each other. He didn't feel that from these boys at all. Still, this was his life now, so he supposed he had to get used to it.

Finally the Weeds ran out of games to play. Flurry immediately curled up and closed his eyes, but he couldn't sleep with so many rocks poking into his fur. Yet it felt good to rest. While he did, he listened to the sound of Quake's and Thunderbolt's voices and imagined they were telling him a bedtime story, just like Winter used to do.

"So what do we do with the bear now?" Quake asked.

"I don't know," Thunderbolt replied. "Do we keep him? I'm kind of getting bored."

"Me too," Quake agreed. "Wish we could use him to get the Sparkles all upset again. That was fun."

"Yeah," Thunderbolt said. "Wait—*yeah*! We're forgetting the best part of this bear!"

"His tail?" Quake asked.

"What? No, not his tail!"

"But it's all small and puffy and cute," Quake said. "What do *you* think is the best part of the bear—his little snout?"

"Just don't talk anymore, okay, Quake?" Thunderbolt said. "The best part of the bear is, he hates the Sparkles just like us. I bet he'd *love* to help us make the Sparkles miserable. And I got an idea just how to do it. Come here, Butch! Come on, ya big ol' bear!"

Flurry got up when he heard the name they liked to call him. He had imagined their conversation was about a present for him—a thick cozy rug to sleep on. He hoped he was right and they'd give him that present right now.

Instead they climbed onto his back again. Thunderbolt pointed a twisted stick at the sky and cried, *"Zzzptzzpsslzzt!"*

A storm cloud floated down until it hovered right in front of Flurry. He sniffed it curiously. He didn't like the smell at all.

"Hop on, Butch," Thunderbolt urged.

The Weed pressed in his heels, so Flurry knew he was supposed to move, but the cloud was in his way. When he tried to step around it, Thunderbolt yelled angrily. He slid off Flurry's back and stood in front of the bear.

"It's real simple, Butchie. I want *you*"—he pointed to Flurry's legs—"up on *that cloud*." Thunderbolt pointed to the wicked-smelling storm cloud. "Just hop on up." The boy leaped forward to show what he meant.

Flurry got it, but he didn't like it. Stepping on a cloud seemed like a very bad idea. Thunderbolt returned to Flurry's back and pressed his heels again, but Flurry needed some more time to think about this.

"*Zzpssszllttss!*" Thunderbolt shouted. Instantly, Flurry felt a shock on his rear end. The electric bolt didn't hurt, but it startled him so badly he jumped, and the storm cloud slipped under him while he was in the air. It whisked Flurry and the Weeds high into the sky.

Flurry shut his eyes and whimpered. He didn't mind heights when he was at the top of a mountain, but standing on a cloud that felt like nothing under his feet? That didn't feel good at all.

The cloud zoomed through the sky so quickly that Flurry's cheeks flapped in the wind. He heard Thunderbolt and Quake laugh and holler. They sounded happy. If they liked the ride so much it couldn't really be dangerous, but Flurry still didn't like it. He wanted it to end.

Suddenly it did. The cloud was gone, and he felt solid ground under his paws. *Cold* solid ground. It reminded him of...

*Home!*

Flurry opened his eyes. He was back in Winter's

Sparkledom! Back with soft snow, beautiful pine trees, and all the smells he loved best. He was so happy he slid the boys off his back and scooped them up into his arms. He hugged them tight and danced with joy.

Quake's face was red from Flurry's tight embrace. "You were right," he squeaked to Thunderbolt. "The bear's as excited to cause trouble as we are."

"A little too excited," Thunderbolt croaked. "*Zzzz-bzztttbbbzt!*"

Another shock tweaked Flurry in the belly. This one didn't hurt either, but it really surprised him. He dropped the boys. His belly tickled a little from the shock, so he threw himself onto a snowbank and writhed around to rub it out. That felt so good that he rolled his whole body around in the snow. He let the fresh coldness erase all traces of the Barrens from his fur.

"Enough of that," Thunderbolt said. "You know where Winter lives, right, Butch? Take us there."

Flurry understood Winter's name, and it made him sad. He was so thrilled to be home, he had

Even though she spoke to all her sisters, she really meant only Summer. Spring was concentrating on Sammy, while Autumn's eyes were shut tight as she tried to cope with the wild ride.

Summer spotted him first. "I see him!" she shouted. "He's running toward your house—and he still has the Weeds!"

"I knew he'd come home!" Winter shouted. "Spring, tell Sammy to bring us down!"

Spring relayed the message and Sammy circled lower. He must have made a lot of noise flapping through the air, because the Weeds looked up when he was still very high. They shouted something none of the Sparkles could hear, then pulled out their wands and aimed them right at Sammy. The sea monster screamed, bucking and twisting until even Winter worried she might be sick.

"What happened?" she cried. "Did they hit him?"

"No!" Spring cried back. "He's afraid they will!"

She leaned close to the sea monster's ear and screeched a series of gurgles and squeals. They hurt Winter's head, but she guessed the sounds must be comforting in Sammy's language.

"It's not helping!" Spring wailed. "He's too scared."

"Then we can't make him stay!" Autumn cried. "Spring, tell him how to get to your lagoon. We'll jump down into the snow."

"We'll . . . *what*?" Winter asked.

It wasn't that she didn't want to jump. She was just shocked *Autumn* suggested it.

"Believe me, I'm not happy about it," Autumn said to Winter, "but it's cruel to keep Sammy anywhere near the Weeds."

Spring was already croaking, wheezing, and squealing instructions to the sea monster.

"It's your Sparkledom," Summer told Winter. "Where's the best place to jump?"

Winter focused on the ground until she saw a snowbank large enough to catch their fall. *"Now!"* she shouted.

All four Sparkles leaped off Sammy's back and tumbled through the air.

*FOOMF! FOOMF! FOOMF! FOOMF!*

They landed with such force that their bodies sank deep in the snow. Winter crawled out easily, then reached back to check the baby fox in her hood.

"You okay back there?" she asked.

Snowball's body shook, but he nuzzled Winter's hand. She didn't need Spring to translate. He was scared, but he was okay.

"You stay cuddled up then," she told him. "I'm going to get my sisters."

The other Sparkles weren't as agile in the snow as Winter. They were still deep in the snowbank. Winter helped them out one by one. "Everybody all right?" she asked.

They nodded.

"Sammy is too," Spring said. "You were all so nice to let him get away, even though it meant we had to jump." Her eyes teared up as she added, "It was the nicest thing I've ever seen anyone do for a sea monster."

"Aww, Spring." Autumn pulled her sister close, and Winter and Summer joined the hug.

"Ain't that sweet?" a raspy voice said. It was Thunderbolt, and he quickly added, "Don't even dream of grabbin' those scepters. You do, and our bear, Butchie, gets it. Look and see, but keep your arms all wrapped around one another so you don't do nothing crazy."

Winter scolded herself. How could she and her sisters be so careless? They *knew* the Weeds were close when they jumped. They should have paid more attention.

With no other choice, the Sparkles obeyed Thunderbolt's order and remained in their hug while they turned to look at the boys. Both Thunderbolt and Quake wore snowshoes cobbled from branches and twigs. Flurry stood between them. Quake had his wand pointed right at the Sparkle Sisters, while Thunderbolt's wand dug into Flurry's side.

"You hurt that bear, Thunderbolt," Winter said, "and I will destroy you."

"Good luck with that," the Weed taunted her. "We've got you all right where we want you."

"Lilies and lilacs!" Spring suddenly gasped. "My scepter! I must have dropped it when we jumped— it's gone!"

The minute she said it, she clamped her hand over her mouth, but it was too late. The boys had heard her, and hungrily scanned the landscape.

"You mean *this* scepter?" Thunderbolt crowed as he ran across the snow and plucked it from the low branches of a pine.

"No!" Spring wailed.

"That's not yours, Thunderbolt! Give it back!" Summer demanded.

"It's mine now." Thunderbolt laughed and tossed the scepter from one hand to the other.

"Please don't throw that," Spring begged. "I don't want it to get hurt."

"Oh, me neither," Thunderbolt said. "In fact, I'd like to see how it works." He pointed the scepter at the Sparkles and shouted his own Weed-y spell.

*"ZZPZZSSSLLLTTT!"*

Black glittery magic shot out of the scepter and disappeared into the snow behind the sisters, but nothing else happened.

"Nice try, Thunderbolt," Winter said, "but Spring's scepter doesn't speak Weed."

Yet even as she said it, a loud rumble filled the air. The snow behind the sisters melted, and the ground bubbled and sparked. Thick, angry plant roots that glowed and snapped with electric energy pushed through the soil and snaked their way toward the Sparkles.

"We need to get out of here," Summer warned. *"Now."*

It was almost as if the electrified roots heard her, because right away, they raced toward the Sparkles at lightning speed and lashed themselves tightly around the girls' ankles, wrists, and waists. The sisters could barely move, and when they did struggle, electric jolts zapped their bodies.

Thunderbolt laughed.

"You make things grow, and I make lightning," he chortled to Spring. "Who knew our powers would mix so perfectly?"

"These roots aren't perfect," Spring said. "They're wicked and horrible!"

"They're also coming this way!" Quake shouted.

It was true. The long electrified roots had trapped the Sparkles, but they didn't stop there. They wanted more victims, and sizzled and snapped their way toward Flurry and the Weeds.

"Hey, that's not cool!" Thunderbolt squealed. He paled and backed feverishly away as Quake and Flurry took cover behind him, but the roots kept coming. "What are you doing hiding behind me?" Thunderbolt cried to his brother and the bear.

"You've got the scepter!" Quake wailed. "Use it!"

"Oh, right." Frantically, Thunderbolt flicked Spring's scepter at the roots and screamed spell after spell, but nothing worked. In seconds the Weeds and bear were surrounded by snapping, sizzling tentacles. Flurry whined and hid his face in his paws. Quake cowered behind his brother. "You gotta do something!" he screamed. "We're gonna get wrapped up like the Sparkles!"

"Not if I can help it," Thunderbolt growled. He stopped shouting spells and smacked Spring's scepter into the roots again and again.

"Stop!" Spring cried. "You'll hurt it!"

"I don't care!" Thunderbolt yelled. And as the roots closed in, he smashed Spring's scepter against them as hard as he possibly could.

The scepter's orb cracked.

The roots froze in place.

"NO!" cried Spring.

Winter's heart stopped. A scepter *broke*! "You'll pay for this, Thunderbolt!" she screamed, and lunged for the Weed, but the roots wrapped around her shocked her back into place.

Thunderbolt laughed. He picked his way around the frozen roots and swaggered toward the Sparkles, Quake and Flurry right behind him. "Nice try," he said. "The roots stopped growing, but they still pack a shock. You're trapped. Which means we can take *all* your scepters. Quake?"

"Me?" Quake asked. "I don't wanna get close to those electrified thingies. What if I touch one and get an owie?"

"QUAKE!" Thunderbolt roared.

"Okay, okay," Quake agreed. He gingerly maneuvered his way around the girls' thick root prison and pulled Summer's, Winter's, and Autumn's scepters from their holsters. The girls could only grit their teeth and watch.

"Got 'em!" Quake crowed. "Bluster's gonna love these!"

"He'll never see them," Winter retorted. "We'll get out of this and stop you long before that."

"Not if our bear can help it," Thunderbolt said. He turned to Flurry. "Now's your chance, Butchie. Get back at Winter *and* her sisters. Pick up this bunch of Sparkles, roots and all, and throw 'em back to our moat in the Barrens."

He acted out what he meant as he said it. Flurry seemed to understand. He stood tall and towered over the Sparkles.

"He won't really do it, will he?" Spring whispered to Winter.

Winter couldn't answer. She had no idea what her bear was thinking. Was he so hurt he'd follow Thunderbolt's orders?

"What's it gonna be, Butchie?" Thunderbolt asked. "Us, or the Sparkle who dumped you when something better came along?"

Flurry set his jaw, then wrapped his arms around the entire tangle of roots encasing the Sparkles. He twisted until it snapped off the ground. A million tiny shocks nipped into each sister's skin as Flurry rose tall on his hind legs and lifted the knot of Sparkles above his head.

"Winter, say something to him," Summer urged.

"On it," Winter whispered. Then she raised her voice and declared, "Flurry, if you want to throw us away, you should."

"Winter, say something *else* to him," Summer hissed.

"I messed up," Winter continued. "You felt like I replaced you, and that's my fault, and I'm sorry. But Flurry, I could *never* replace you. Ever. You're my best friend in the world. Nothing and no one can ever change that. But if you don't feel the same way . . . then go ahead and throw me away, because I don't want to be here if I have to be here without you."

Endless moments passed as Winter and Flurry stared into each other's eyes. Autumn, Spring, and Summer watched anxiously, barely daring to breathe.

Then Flurry roared. He cocked his arms back behind his head, ready to hurl the Sparkles as far as he could.

Winter and her sisters closed their eyes and waited for the worst.

## CHAPTER
# 10

*C*RUNCH!

Flurry squeezed the electrified roots between his paws, crumbling them to stinging bits. The Sparkles fell to the snowy ground, but Winter leaped up immediately and hugged Flurry tight.

"I love you, Flurry!" Winter cried. "I knew you wouldn't give up on us."

"Touching," Quake said, and they all spun to see the three unbroken Sparkle scepters pointed right at them. "Just stay where you are, understand? I don't want to use these, but I will if I have to. Hey, Thunderbolt," he called to his brother, "how's that getaway cloud coming?"

"Almost here," Thunderbolt replied. He stood behind Quake and used his own wand to guide a storm cloud down from the sky.

"What do we do?" Winter asked her sisters.

"Tackle them," Summer said.

"Done," Winter said. "Flurry will help."

"No," Autumn said, "no tackling. If we move, Quake will use the scepters. His powers mixed with all three of ours? We have no idea what could happen."

"So we just let them take our scepters away?" Spring asked.

No one answered. There was nothing to say.

Then Flurry dropped down to all fours and grumbled curiously.

"What do you mean?" Winter asked. Flurry nodded his head, and Winter followed his gaze to see Snowball, the baby fox. Winter hadn't even felt him climb out of her hood, but now he was trotting toward Quake and Thunderbolt.

He barked and wagged his tail.

"Shut it!" Thunderbolt snapped. "I'm tryin' to concentrate here!" His storm cloud was very close to the ground. Another minute, and he and Quake could hop on and zoom away with the scepters.

Snowball barked again. He did one backflip, then another.

Quake had his eye on the Sparkles, but he couldn't help but notice the pup's performance. "Hey, Thunderbolt, you gotta see this."

Winter smiled. She wrapped an arm around Flurry's neck and leaned close to his ear. "I've got a good feeling about this," she said. "Get ready."

Snowball yipped, did two more backward flips, two forward flips, then rolled over. Quake was only half paying attention to the Sparkles now, and Thunderbolt was so impressed that he turned away from his storm cloud to watch.

"That's pretty good!" he said. "Hey, foxie, you wanna come live with us?"

"Yeah!" Quake said. "We'll call you Butchie Two!"

Snowball rolled onto his back and waved his paws in the air.

"Awwww!" chorused Quake and Thunderbolt. Both boys knelt down and dropped everything in their hands so they could rub Snowball's belly.

"*Now*, Flurry," Winter whispered.

In a flash, Flurry tucked two claws through the

backs of Quake's and Thunderbolt's collars, then stood to his full height. The boys kicked and twisted in the air while the Sparkles scrambled to pick up their scepters.

"HEY!" Thunderbolt shouted. "Not fair!"

"Yeah," Quake agreed. "Put us down!"

"Done," Winter declared. "Flurry, put them down . . . in the Barrens."

The boys shouted their objections, but Flurry didn't hesitate. He drew back his paws and hurled the Weeds far out of sight. Winter wasn't worried for them. She knew her bear had a kind heart and great aim. The two boys would land somewhere safe and sound but very far away. She picked up their wands and handed them to Flurry. "Here," she said. "Send these after them."

"Hold up," Summer objected. "Shouldn't we keep the wands? They'd keep ours."

"Exactly," Winter said. "But we're not them. Right, Flurry?"

The bear answered by hurling the wands after the Weeds. Then he dropped back to all fours and rubbed up against Winter so energetically he almost knocked her over. Winter didn't mind at all.

"Bark!"

Winter and Flurry both looked down to see Snowball prancing at their feet. Winter smiled at the pup, then looked nervously to Flurry. "So, about Snowball here . . ."

Flurry crouched down low, nose-to-nose with the baby fox. He glared.

Snowball whimpered.

"Dahlias and daffodils," Spring whispered nervously. "Will Flurry hurt him?"

Just then Flurry pounced . . . and gave Snowball a giant tongue-lick kiss that soaked the tiny pup from head to toe. Snowball shook himself dry, then leaped onto Flurry's head, where he cuddled into the bear's snowy fur. Flurry smiled and swayed side to side, rocking the baby to sleep.

"I don't believe it," Winter said. "I think Flurry wants to keep him."

"He's not the only one," Summer said. "Look!"

She pointed to a group of trees, from which a

family of two grown-up foxes and two babies had emerged. An adult fox barked, and Snowball bolted upright. He leaped off Flurry's head and ran to his family, barking excitedly. Soon all five were cuddling, leaping, and rolling together in the snow.

"Awwww," Spring cooed. "Snowball's family is so

happy to see him! They've been looking for him since the blizzard, and they have so much to tell him. Cousin Lucy caught a cold, and Snowball's brother and sister went ice-sliding with penguins, and ... really!"

Spring barked, yipped, and growled at the fox family. All except Snowball stared at her a moment, as if stunned she spoke their language. Then they all crowded around her, barking, yipping, and growling excitedly. Spring went wide-eyed as she took in the conversation. "No, he didn't . . . he couldn't . . . he *did*? That's so *sweet*!" Spring turned to her sisters. "The foxes say thank you for taking such good care of Snowball. They hope we can all play again soon."

"What do you think, Flurry?" Winter asked. "*Can* we all play again soon?"

Flurry frowned and plopped sulkily down into the snow.

"Let me guess," Winter said, "you'd rather we all play *now*?"

Flurry leaped to his feet and did a booty-shaking dance. Snowball joined in, and the Sparkles laughed out loud.

Suddenly the sound of wind chimes filled the air. A warm breeze blew, and everything smelled like a mix of apples, ocean air, pine needles, and flowers. A thrill ran through Winter, and she locked eyes with each of her sisters. They all knew who was coming, and Winter knew their hearts were beating faster just like hers. Soon a wide column of millions of tiny rainbow-colored crystals appeared in front of them. The crystals danced in shimmering swirls, and everything in Winter's Sparkledom seemed to lean toward them. Even Winter leaned forward, and the closer she got, the happier she felt.

With a *poof!* of rainbow-colored smoke, the crystals vanished. In their place stood the Sparkles' mom, Mother Nature.

"Mother!" Winter cried.

Winter, Summer, and Autumn all raced to her and wrapped their arms around her. Mother hugged all three of them equally, so no one felt left out.

"Hmmm," she said. "Something's missing from this Sparkle hug. Spring?"

Spring kept her sad eyes on the ground. With a shaking hand, she held out her cracked scepter.

"It wasn't her fault," Winter told Mother.

"Thunderbolt did it," Summer added.

"And Spring was so brave," Autumn added. "We met a monster in the Barrens and—"

"Sammy," Mother said. "Yes, he and I just had a

lovely visit. Pink Dolphin Lagoon was an excellent choice. He'll be very happy there. As for this . . ."

Mother bent down to examine Spring's scepter orb. It was always a beautiful violet, or shaded by the silver mist that signaled the season's end, but now it had no color at all.

"I'm sorry, Mother," Spring said in barely a whisper.

Mother put a finger under Spring's chin and lifted it. "You don't have to be," she said. "Sometimes, despite our best intentions, things go wrong and things crack. But in many cases, if it's something you truly love—like perhaps a friendship—you'll find it can always be repaired."

Mother leaned so close to Spring that the gem in Mother's tiara touched the gem in Spring's head-band. Rainbow sparkles glowed in the spot where the two gems met, then flowed down the side of Spring's head, along her arm, and into her scepter. When the sparkles reached Spring's scepter orb, they flashed so brightly that all the sisters had to look away.

When they looked back, the scepter wasn't cracked at all, and it glowed a beautiful violet once more.

"Thank you, Mother!" Spring hurled herself into her arms.

"You're very welcome," Mother replied. Then she turned to Winter with a smile. "So am I wrong, or is your kitchen baking gingerbread?"

"You're right. I smell it too!" Winter said. "Which makes it the perfect time for a gingerbread party at my house! We'll celebrate friends—old friends and new ones too."

"I thought you might say that," Mother said, "which is why I extended another invitation."

A gurgling roar pierced the air and everyone looked up to see . . .

"Sammy!"

The monster landed gently, and although Flurry and the foxes were startled by him at first, Sammy quickly won them over by taking mouthfuls of snow and shooting them out of his blowhole to make flurries—an impressive trick the Sparkles had never seen before.

As they all trooped together to Winter's home, Winter felt warmer inside than a mug of hot chocolate. Just a few hours ago she thought she had lost her best friend, but now she knew the truth: real friendship can work through anything and come out stronger than ever before.

Winter looked around at everyone she loved. She felt perfectly happy and was positive she'd never appreciated her friends and family more than she did right now.

She promised herself she always would.

**Elise Allen** is the author of the young adult novel *Populazzi* and the chapter book *Anna's Icy Adventure*, based on Disney's *Frozen*. She cowrote the *New York Times* bestselling Elixir trilogy with Hilary Duff, and the Autumn Falls series with Bella Thorne. A longtime collaborator with the Jim Henson Company, she's written for *Sid the Science Kid* and *Dinosaur Train*.
www.eliseallen.com

**Halle Stanford**, an eight-time Emmy-nominated children's television producer, is in charge of creating children's entertainment at the Jim Henson Company. She currently serves as the executive producer on the award-winning series *Sid the Science Kid*, *Dinosaur Train*, *Pajanimals*, and *Doozers*.

**Paige Pooler** is an artist who loves to draw pictures for girls. You can find Paige's artwork in *American Girl* magazine and the Liberty Porter, Trading Faces, and My Sister the Vampire middle grade series.
www.paigepooler.com

**The Jim Henson Company** has remained an established leader in family entertainment for over fifty years and is the creator of such Emmy-nominated hits as *Sid the Science Kid*, *Dinosaur Train*, *Pajanimals*, and *Fraggle Rock*. The company is currently developing the Enchanted Sisters series as an animated TV property.
www.henson.com